A Bee to Remember

by Kerrian Neu

First published by AuthorHouse 03/17/05

ISBN: 1-4208-3653-6 (sc)

Library of Congress Control Number: 2005902382

Printed in the United States of America
Bloomington, Indiana

This book is printed on acid-free paper.

authorHOUSE

1663 LIBERTY DRIVE
BLOOMINGTON, INDIANA 47403
(800) 839-8640
www.authorhouse.com

Hi, I'm Ben the Bee, *Official Junior Bee Detective.* I live in the town of Beely - population 492. My dad is the Chief Policebee and he lets me and Scooter *(my assistant)* help on some cases.

Being a good Official Junior Bee Detective, this is my report for Case #142, *A Bee to Remember.*

SATURDAY: MORNING

It was a busy day in Beely. Everyone was preparing the town for the world premier of the movie, *"A Bee to Remember"* and the arrival of it's stars, Abbee Honeybee and Timothy Lockabee.

Mr. Tobee, owner of the HoneyComb Grill, cleaned all of his windows.

Mr. Goodbee, owner of the Beely Market, a long established family business, brought fresh goods to the inn.

Miss Penny Parsley, owner of the Broken Pot Café, picked lots of flowers.

Jonny Bumble, who owns the Bumble Bar, swept all the floors.

At the Burnt Tree Inn, Mr. Whetherbee dusted everything in sight.

Eddy from the Beely Bowl, and May Bee,
who works at the HoneyComb Grill,
hung the 'Welcome' sign on the Courthouse.

And Buzzy, the local golf pro
at Clover Fields Golf Course,
stayed busy stacking golf balls.

SATURDAY: AFTERNOON

Movie stars, Abbee Honeybee and Timothy Lockabee arrived at the Burnt Tree Inn amidst much fanfare. There were more photographers than I, Ben, an Official Junior Bee Detective, can ever remember seeing in Beely!

Maribee, who is movie star Abbee's assistant, lagged behind, bringing Abbee's luggage to the inn.

SATURDAY: EARLY EVENING

According to Mr. Whetherbee, the Burnt Tree Inn Manager, before going to the premier, Abbee ordered room-service from the inn.

May Bee brought the dinner to the room. She was very nervous and excited to meet Abbee Honeybee, her favorite actress.

When May Bee got close to the table, she was even more nervous. She started to shake; she also noticed Abbee's beautiful necklace, got distracted, and spilled everything all over the table, the floor and Abbee!

As May Bee apologized and tried to clean up the mess, Maribee ordered her to leave the room immediately. So May Bee left without taking the mess with her.

Much to his distress, Mr. Whetherbee had to clean it up before going to the premier.

SATURDAY: NIGHT-TIME

The whole town of Beely came out for the world premier of *"A Bee to Remember"*. Abbee Honeybee and Timothy Lockabee were greeted by Queen Rose. My parents, Chief Charlie and Elise were there.

My mom said it was for adults. Only Tony, a kid from school who always picks on me and works part-time at the drive inn was there, *(since it is his job)* to pass out tickets to the movie.

SUNDAY: MORNING

My dad, Chief Charlie, was called to the Burnt Tree Inn first thing Sunday morning. Abbee Honeybee was very upset. She could not find her prized necklace anywhere. It had been her Grandmother's and was also very valuable.

Abbee's assistant, Maribee, wanted to leave Beely immediately. She even started to pack, but Abbee refused to budge without her necklace.

My dad promised to get on the case and wrote down all the vital information Abbee could remember from the night before. He told her not to worry; her necklace would be found.

Maribee said she doubted it would ever be found and still insisted that they leave Beely right away anyway. Dad told me that she seemed pretty negative towards the town.

My Dad returned home after leaving the Burnt Tree Inn and filing his report at the police station. He thought that Scooter *(my trusty assistant and best friend)* and I would be perfect detectives for the case, since most of his deputies were busy with other important investigations. We were outside on the porch reading our favorite comics; Scooter - *Alien Bee Antics,* and me - *The Adventures of Super Bee,* a very good tale of a hero vs. evil, where Dad found us and told us about Abbee's missing necklace. Since I am an Official Junior Bee Detective, Scooter and I were officially on the case.

<u>SUNDAY: LUNCH TIME</u>

Being the good Official Junior Bee Detective I am, our first stop was the Broken Pot Café. Any good detective knows that a restaurant is a great place to get information, and besides, we were *really* hungry for Clover Burgers and Honey Fries. Miss Penny Parsley makes the best fries, and Scooter has a crush on her. While feasting on our burgers, we could hear other people talking about the premier and the party afterwards.

"...I saw Abbee sneak out into the Clover Fields during the party..."

"...I danced with Timothy last night. Abbee seemed jealous..."

"...Her assistant was rude to me..."

"...Abbee looks prettier in person..."

"...This burger is really good..."

"...I saw Abbee going towards the Flower Pots..."

SUNDAY: AFTER BURGERS

Since we heard Abbee had gone to the Clover Fields outside of the Burnt Tree Inn, Scooter and I headed there first. We checked around all the clover trunks and up their stems, but found nothing.

Scooter and I deduced there wasn't anything there, *(plus Scooter thought it was kind of spooky)* and headed next for the Flower Pots.

Flowers are grown to harvest the pollen to make honey, Beely's major industry, at the Flower Pots.

Scooter and I searched and searched through the flower stems of the first pot we came to. We were just about to move on, when I spotted something sparkling in the sunlight - part of the missing necklace!

I couldn't believe we were so lucky to find a clue so fast!

Scooter and I figured the rest of the necklace had to be close, so it would be best to check the other flower pots, but Scooter and I found nothing else and it was getting later in the day. Then we heard voices in the last pot! Since I'm an Official Junior Bee Detective, I knew that we should get close enough to see and hear who was there, but not close enough to be seen.

Henry and Herb Comb, who own Comb Bro's Honey Manufacturing were there talking discreetly to a tall stranger! We couldn't hear what they were saying, but it seemed odd that the Comb brothers were there, since they rarely left their homes or the Honey Manufacturing plant.

MONDAY: MATH CLASS

The day started with school. During math class, Daisy, my other best friend, wanted to hear about our investigation. Daisy sometimes assists with cases, even though she is usually really busy with other activities. I told her about some of what we learned so far, but a good detective never tells everything. Tony, who always picks on Scooter and me, started to tease us about the investigation. Daisy wanted to hear more, so we decided to talk later when Tony wasn't around.

<u>MONDAY: AFTERNOON</u>

After school, Scooter and I met up with Daisy. She really wanted to help us, so she brought along her pet flea, Spot. Spot is a good flea; he can sniff-out clues.

Our first stop of the afternoon was to see Mr. Goodbee at the
Beely Market. He knows everyone in town and always
gives us candy. Mr. Goodbee didn't know anything about the
missing necklace though. At least we all got a stick
of candy *(except for Spot, of course)*.

We went outside the Beely Market to eat our candy and to discuss our next move. Dad came by with some photos from the night of the premier. He thought we would like to take a look at them as a part of our investigation.

Spot rolled around and laid in the sun; he wasn't much help to the case.

Photos:

Abbee with Timothy and Maribee checking in at the Burnt Tree Inn.

Abbee and Queen Rose at the movie premier.

Abbee talking to my mom at the premier party.

My parents dancing behind Abbee and Timothy dancing at the party. No necklace! Her necklace went missing at the party!

TUESDAY: AFTERNOON
Since we had homework on Monday, we postponed our investigation until the next day after school.

Scooter and I decided to see how Mr. Whetherbee was at the Burnt Tree Inn. He was still very upset about the loss of the necklace, dropped all his papers and couldn't say anything that made sense. He get's flustered rather easily, but he is fun to talk to.

Room 301:

We next went to talk with Abbee's assistant, Maribee. She answered the door, but was quite angry and wouldn't let us in. She told us to leave her and Abbee alone.

Apparently Maribee was still upset about having to staying in Beely. Scooter and I were definitely shocked by her attitude. She slammed the door shut before we even turned to leave!

Since we were getting nowhere trying to interview Maribee, Scooter and I decided to go to the ballroom, where the party had been. Workerbees were still cleaning up when we got there. Mr. Whetherbee didn't let them start to clean the room until today. We were just about to leave, but then Scooter spotted the stranger from the Flower Pots! We knew we needed to follow him and find out more about him.

We followed the stranger through the streets of the town, into the post office and finally to the Hive Apartment Towers. Since I'm a good detective, we kept a safe distance between us and him so we would not be spotted. As we watched him, the stranger entered one of the Hive Apartment Towers.

<u>TUESDAY: EARLY EVENING</u>
Scooter and I decided to wait
  outside the Towers for the
  stranger to leave.

We waited...

and waited...

and waited...

and waited.

Scooter fell asleep and I was
tired of waiting. It was also
getting late, so I woke up
Scooter and we called it
a night.

TUESDAY: DINNER TIME

Dinner was spaghetti and clover balls, my favorite!

Mom asked how the investigation was going. I told her about Abbee's angry assistant, Mr. Whetherbee and the stranger from the Flower Pots who we saw in the ballroom and at the Hive Apartment Towers. Dad said it would be best for me to stay away from the stranger until he could identify him. Mom told both Dad and I to be careful.

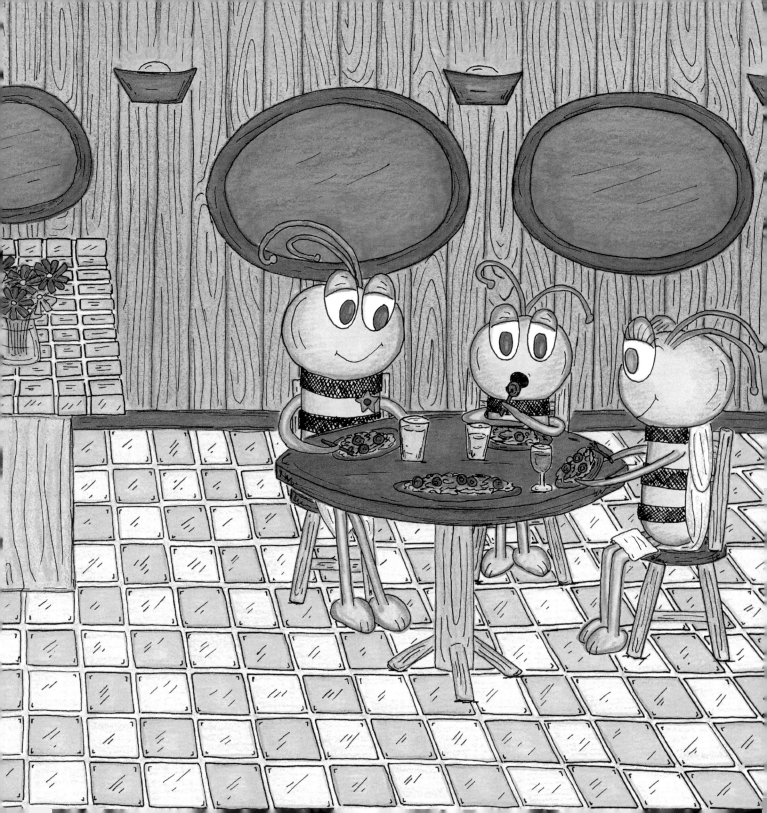

<u>WEDNESDAY: AFTER SCHOOL</u>

We began our next day of investigating with a couple scoops of ice cream from Mr. Goodbee. It seemed like a good place to start, and Scooter was hungry.

Dad came by *(somehow he knows we always start our investigations at the Beely Market)* and told me that the stranger was in fact Haley Comb, the son of Henry Comb. He's back in town and working at the Hive Bottling Company.

Scooter didn't hear our conversation, because he dropped a scoop of his ice cream on the ground. *(He always drops at least one scoop!)*

After I informed Scooter about the stranger and we finished our ice cream, we headed to question Haley Comb at the Hive Bottling Company. Haley would only tell us that he knew Abbee when he was in college and just wanted to see her again. When I asked what he was doing at the ballroom yesterday, he told us to leave him alone.

Another suspect had refused to talk with us.

WEDNESDAY: LATE AFTERNOON

Since our investigation yielded no good leads, we headed to the Beely Police Station to see more of the photos from the night of the premier. Scooter got bored fairly quickly, but finally I found a photo that when you looked close enough, you could see Abbee's assistant, Maribee, holding the necklace!

Being a good Official Junior Bee Detective, I immediately informed my dad. Dad was busy with his police work, so Scooter and I decided to have a talk with Maribee on our own.

We arrived at the inn and ran up to Maribee's room. No one answered our knock, so I discreetly turned the door handle, and the door opened easily. Scooter started looking in drawers; I searched under the bed, where I found Maribee's partially packed suitcase. We pulled it out, opened the lid, and started searching inside.

All of a sudden, Maribee appeared behind us. She grabbed Scooter around his neck and said we would be sorry for being so nosey. I looked for a way to stop Maribee, who was now trying to choke Scooter. She gave me a sharp kick in the leg and I fell down. We were in deep trouble.

WEDNESDAY: EARLY EVENING

Suddenly a knock was heard at the Maribee's door. Maribee dropped Scooter, who was now gasping for air, slammed her suitcase shut, and headed for the bathroom window. In the same instant, the door burst open and Dad and one of his deputies came bursting in. His deputy grabbed Maribee before she or her suitcase could make it out the window, and handcuffed her. Dad opened her suitcase, where at the very bottom, he found the missing piece of the necklace.

Maribee, proclaimed her innocence and declared she must have been framed by a deranged fan out to get her job. She ranted all the way to the police station, claiming to be innocent.

FRIDAY: AFTER SCHOOL

Abbee Honeybee liked Beely so much she decided to stay a couple extra days. Abbee was very grateful that Scooter and I helped in the recovery of her necklace and called us her heros. She told us it had been in her family for several generations, and she was shocked that her assistant would take it.

Maribee was taken away to the Cloverburg Prison this morning. *(Scooter heard that May Bee was trying to become Abbee's new assistant).* Scooter and I took pictures with Abbee, and Queen Rose gave us her congratulations. It was a great afternoon.

<u>SATURDAY</u>

Today, Dad took Scooter and me for ice cream by the river. He told us that Maribee finally confessed to taking Abbee's necklace and the reason why she took it was that she wanted to sell it to make some extra money. Maribee said she figured that Abbee would have wanted to leave Beely immediately and nobody would find out she was responsible for the theft.

Dad said that crime doesn't ever pay, especially since he always catches the criminals. He also told us to be more careful in the future, and to never take unnecessary risks. Then he told us some more stories about when he first became a policebee. Scooter and I just listened, ate our ice cream and watched the water flow by.

Beely - population 492

SPECIAL THANKS TO

My parents - who helped with all the finishing touches, and whose love and continuous support have allowed me to explore the world of Ben the Bee.

All my friends and family - who have inspired characters as well as the names of the citizens of Beely, especially:

Gary and Tricia (the original Sparkle!), Ed and Sharon, Dan and Joan, Carol and Jeff